1

A PARRAGON BOOK

PUBLISHED BY PARRAGON BOOK SERVICE LTD.
UNITS 13-17, AVONBRIDGE TRADING ESTATE, ATLANTIC ROAD,
AVONMOUTH, BRISTOL BS11 9QD

PRODUCED BY THE TEMPLAR COMPANY PLC,
PIPPBROOK MILL, LONDON ROAD, DORKING, SURREY RH4 1JE

COPYRIGHT © 1996 PARRAGON BOOK SERVICE LIMITED

DESIGNED BY MARK KINGSLEY-MONKS

ILLUSTRATED BY HELEN COCKBURN

PRINTED AND BOUND IN SPAIN

ISBN 0-75252-034-2

CHILDREN'S STORYTIME TREASURY

Tales from the Arabian Nights

CHILDREN'S STORYTIME TREASURY

Tales from the Arabian Nights

PARRAGON

Ali Baba and the Forty Thieves

Far away in the land of Persia there lived two brothers, Ali Baba and Cassim. Ali Baba was a poor man but Cassim was wealthy and lived in a fine house with plenty to eat and drink. Sadly, his wife was a greedy woman and always wanted more.

Ali Baba was chopping firewood in the forest one day when he heard the sound of horse's hooves. He feared that robbers might be coming so scrambled up a tree to safety. Silently he watched as a large body of men rode past and pulled up by a sheer rock face. The leader of the men dismounted and strode up to the rock.

"Open, Sesame!" he cried, and to Ali Baba's great amazement a secret door swung open. Ali Baba counted as the men slipped inside the opening and disappeared from view.

"Forty robbers!" he said to himself. "I wonder what they have hidden inside that cave." Some time later the robbers emerged and galloped away. Then Ali Baba slid down from the tree and stood by the rock face.

"Open, Sesame!" he cried, and lo and behold, the rock door slid open and he quickly ran inside.

Ali Baba expected to find a dark and dismal hole but to his great astonishment the cave was full of the most magnificent treasures. Fine silks lay in bundles upon the floor and exquisite jewels were scattered round about. Great coffers and chests overflowed with gold coins and yet more gold was heaped up in piles around the walls. Ali Baba rubbed his hands with glee! Now he need never go hungry again. Quickly he gathered up as much gold as he could carry and hurried home.

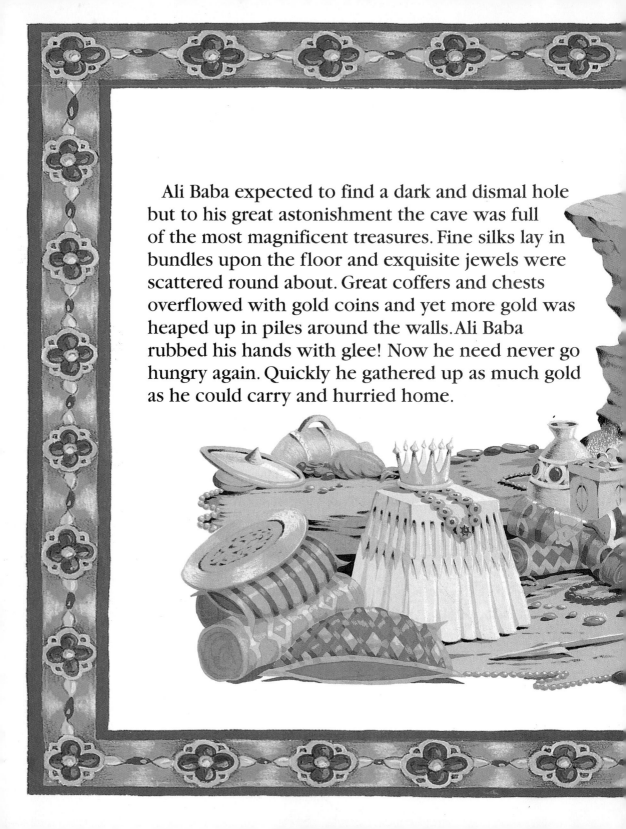

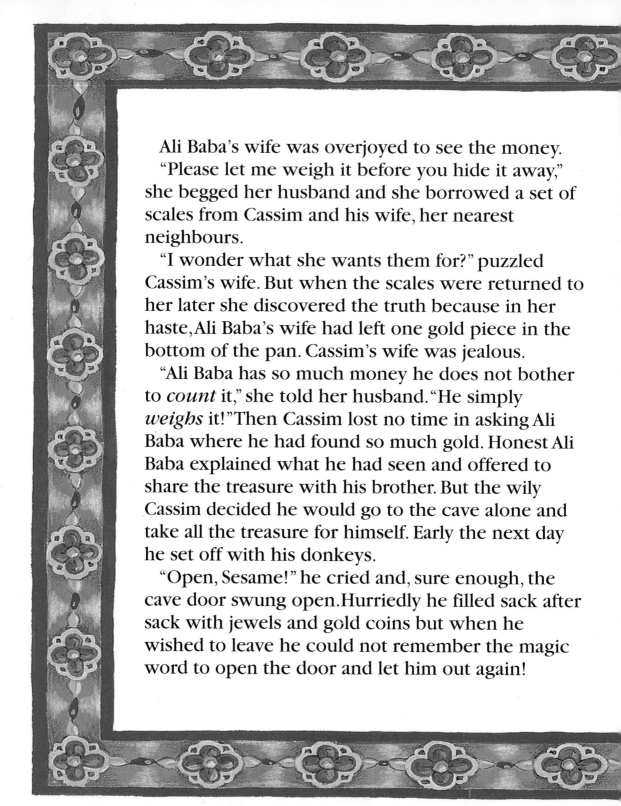

Ali Baba's wife was overjoyed to see the money.

"Please let me weigh it before you hide it away," she begged her husband and she borrowed a set of scales from Cassim and his wife, her nearest neighbours.

"I wonder what she wants them for?" puzzled Cassim's wife. But when the scales were returned to her later she discovered the truth because in her haste, Ali Baba's wife had left one gold piece in the bottom of the pan. Cassim's wife was jealous.

"Ali Baba has so much money he does not bother to *count* it," she told her husband. "He simply *weighs* it!" Then Cassim lost no time in asking Ali Baba where he had found so much gold. Honest Ali Baba explained what he had seen and offered to share the treasure with his brother. But the wily Cassim decided he would go to the cave alone and take all the treasure for himself. Early the next day he set off with his donkeys.

"Open, Sesame!" he cried and, sure enough, the cave door swung open. Hurriedly he filled sack after sack with jewels and gold coins but when he wished to leave he could not remember the magic word to open the door and let him out again!

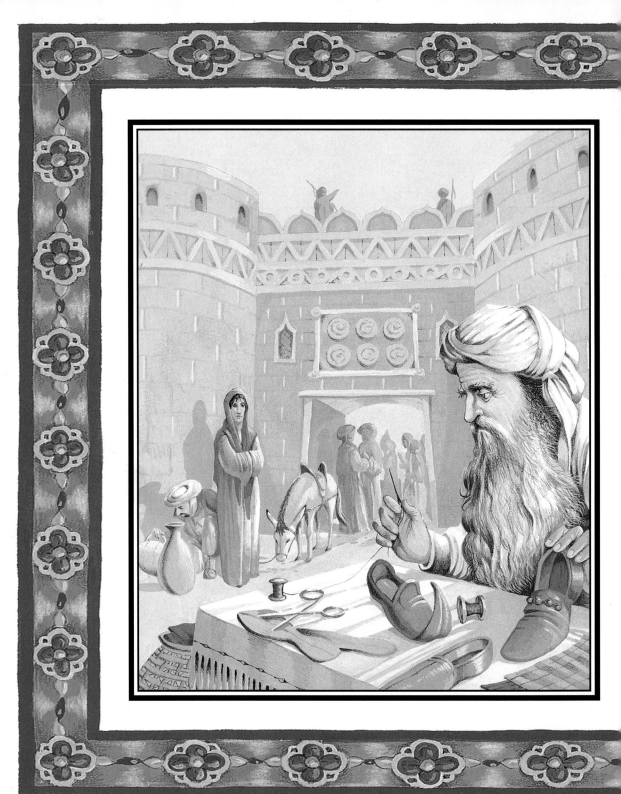

Cassim tried name after name but the door stayed firmly shut. After a while, to his great horror, he heard the trampling of horse's hooves outside the cave. In rushed the robbers and they fell upon him with their long sabres and cut him into four quarters. Then they left him there as a lesson to any other intruder.

That night Ali Baba went in search of Cassim and what a dreadful sight awaited him when he entered the cave. Sadly, he carried home the four quarters of his body and laid them on the table. Cassim's wife wailed and sobbed but Ali Baba's servant, a clever woman called Morgiana, remained calm.

"I will find a cobbler to stitch the four quarters together," she decided, "and then the body can be buried peacefully." So saying, she set off for the market and there she found an old cobbler hard at work.

"I have a job for you, old man," she whispered, "but you must not breathe a word of it to anyone." Then she tied a blindfold around his head and led him to the house of Ali Baba. The cobbler stitched away at the four quarters and late that night Morgiana blindfolded him once more and led him back to his stall.

When the Forty Thieves returned to their cave they were astonished to find that the body was missing.

"Someone else knows our secret password!" cried the Captain. "He must be found!" One of the robbers was sent to the city to discover all he could and as he entered the city gate the first person he saw was the old cobbler. When the robber offered him a gold coin, the cobbler told him all that had happened.

"I am sure I could find the house again," he said and soon he had led the robber to the very door.

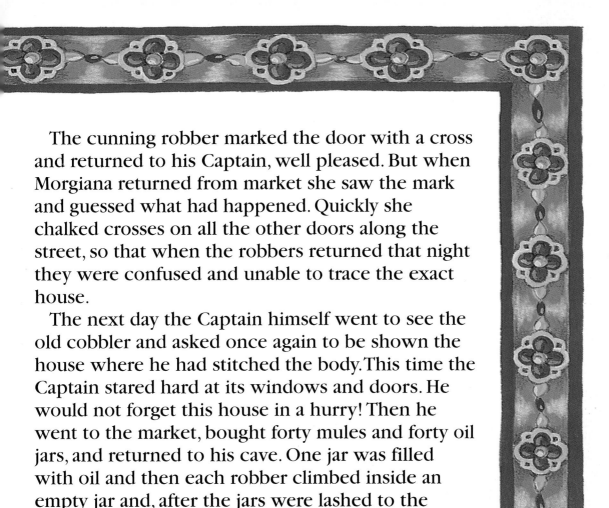

The cunning robber marked the door with a cross and returned to his Captain, well pleased. But when Morgiana returned from market she saw the mark and guessed what had happened. Quickly she chalked crosses on all the other doors along the street, so that when the robbers returned that night they were confused and unable to trace the exact house.

The next day the Captain himself went to see the old cobbler and asked once again to be shown the house where he had stitched the body. This time the Captain stared hard at its windows and doors. He would not forget this house in a hurry! Then he went to the market, bought forty mules and forty oil jars, and returned to his cave. One jar was filled with oil and then each robber climbed inside an empty jar and, after the jars were lashed to the mules' backs, they set off for the city.

Disguised as an oil merchant, the Captain stopped outside Ali Baba's house and knocked on the door.

"I am taking my oil to sell at the market tomorrow," he said, "but now I need somewhere to stay the night. Can you help me?" Kind Ali Baba invited him inside and sent the mules to be stabled in the yard.

Later that night the Captain crept into the yard and whispered his orders to his men, still hiding in the jars.

"Be ready to fight when I give you the word!" he hissed, then tiptoed back inside to join his host. Ali Baba had invited him to join them for a meal and Morgiana was busy cooking in the kitchen.

"I was not expecting visitors," she fussed to herself, "and now I have run out of oil!" Then she remembered the oil jars in the yard. "I am sure the merchant will not mind if a take a little for my cooking," she said to herself as she hurried outside with her jar and lamp. Suddenly she heard a voice — and she was sure it came from inside one of the oil jars!

"Is it time to fight yet, master?" it said. Then Morgiana knew that these were the robbers come to attack her master and, filling her lamp with oil, she quickly ran back inside the house. She boiled a large pan of oil and when it was scalding hot she tipped it over each of the robbers until they were all dead.

At midnight the Captain tried to rouse his robbers but without success. When he discovered each one had been killed he fled over the wall and was gone.

The next morning Morgiana told Ali Baba of all that had happened and he thanked the clever girl for saving his life. But back in the lonely cave, the Robber Captain sat hatching a different plot to kill him.

This time he disguised himself as a rich cloth merchant and set up a stall opposite Ali Baba's house. As the days passed the unsuspecting Ali Baba grew quite friendly with the merchant and invited him to dine at his house.

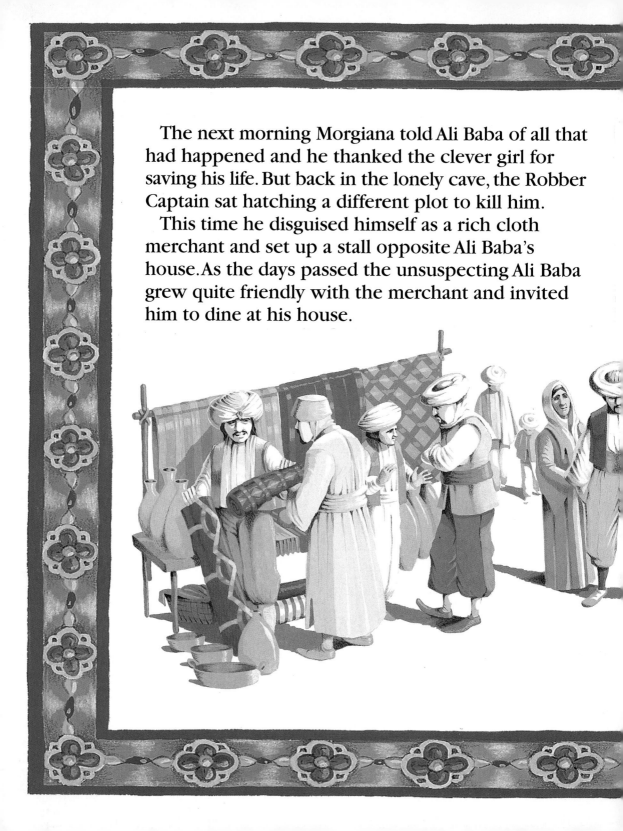

But as soon as the merchant arrived at the door clever Morgiana knew who it was straight away.

"Fetch your drum!" she told Abdallah, the kitchen servant. "I will dance for my master and his honoured guest." Ali Baba, his son and the pretend merchant lay upon silk cushions on the floor. As the drum beat grew louder, Morgiana whirled around the room, each time coming ever closer to the wicked Robber Captain.

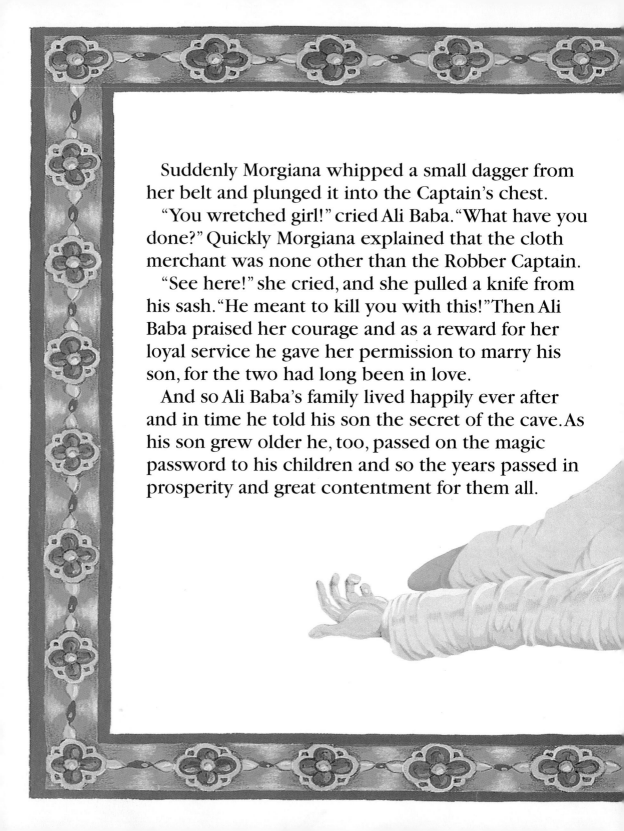

Suddenly Morgiana whipped a small dagger from her belt and plunged it into the Captain's chest.

"You wretched girl!" cried Ali Baba. "What have you done?" Quickly Morgiana explained that the cloth merchant was none other than the Robber Captain.

"See here!" she cried, and she pulled a knife from his sash. "He meant to kill you with this!" Then Ali Baba praised her courage and as a reward for her loyal service he gave her permission to marry his son, for the two had long been in love.

And so Ali Baba's family lived happily ever after and in time he told his son the secret of the cave. As his son grew older he, too, passed on the magic password to his children and so the years passed in prosperity and great contentment for them all.

Aladdin and the Magic Lamp

O nce upon a time there lived a lazy boy called
Aladdin. His father was dead and his poor
mother despaired of her good-for-nothing
son ever finding himself a job for he spent all his
time running around the street markets and teasing
the stallholders. One day a stranger approached him.
"Are you Aladdin?" he asked, and the boy nodded.

"I am your father's brother and have been away for a long time," explained the man. "Now I am back and would like to give you work." When Aladdin's mother heard this news she was overjoyed and welcomed the stranger to their home. But what the trusting woman did not know was that this was no uncle but a scheming magician who was looking for a boy to help him.

"I will buy you some new clothes," said the pretend uncle to Aladdin, "and then you must come with me on a short journey." The next day they walked for many miles into the country and soon the town was left far behind. The boy's feet ached and he longed to go back.

"We are here," said the magician at last and he made a small fire. Throwing on some strange powders, he chanted a magic spell and the earth trembled under their feet. To Aladdin's astonishment a stone slab appeared in the ground. The magician pulled it back to reveal a flight of steps leading down and out of sight.

"You are to follow the steps into a secret garden and there you will find a lamp," said the magician. "Bring it to me and I will reward you well." Then he gave the boy a ring. "Wear this for protection," he said.

The Garden was full of beautiful trees sparkling with the strangest fruit Aladdin had ever seen.

"I will take some home with me," he said, then he found the lamp and returned to the top of the steps.

"Hand me the lamp and you can come out," ordered the magician and his eyes glittered cruelly. Aladdin shivered. He did not trust this man.

"First give me my reward," he insisted. The magician had not expected this and he flew into a rage.

"Do you not know who I am, you foolish boy?" he cried and he slammed the stone slab shut. Then the angry magician fled far away to Africa, leaving poor Aladdin trapped in the dark cave. For two whole days the boy wept bitterly then at last he fell to his knees and prayed for help. His fingers rubbed the ring and suddenly a huge genie appeared in front of him.

"What is your wish?" thundered the genie. "I am the Slave of the Ring and will obey you in all things."

Aladdin lost no time in wishing to be taken home and soon found himself back with his mother.

"Why would the wicked man want this dirty old lamp?" she wondered and she gave it a rub.

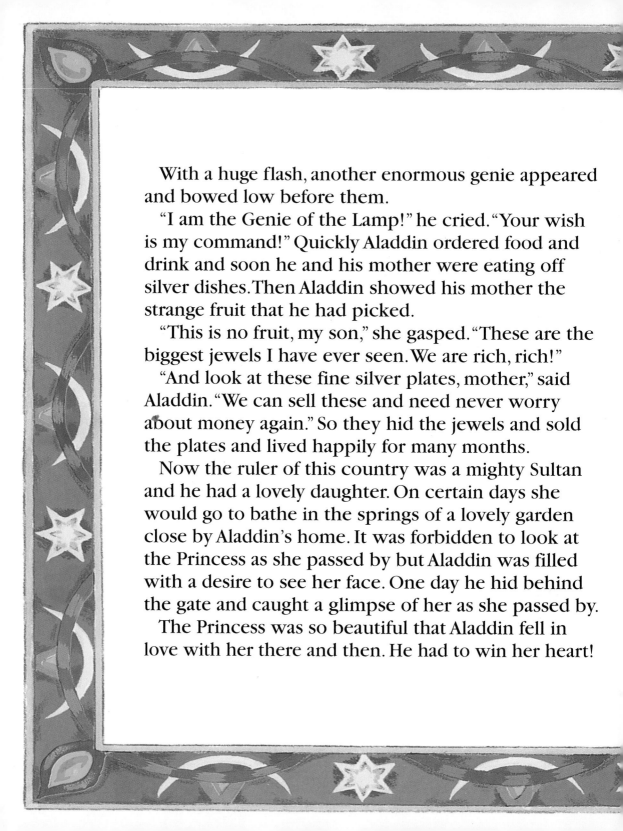

With a huge flash, another enormous genie appeared and bowed low before them.

"I am the Genie of the Lamp!" he cried. "Your wish is my command!" Quickly Aladdin ordered food and drink and soon he and his mother were eating off silver dishes. Then Aladdin showed his mother the strange fruit that he had picked.

"This is no fruit, my son," she gasped. "These are the biggest jewels I have ever seen. We are rich, rich!"

"And look at these fine silver plates, mother," said Aladdin. "We can sell these and need never worry about money again." So they hid the jewels and sold the plates and lived happily for many months.

Now the ruler of this country was a mighty Sultan and he had a lovely daughter. On certain days she would go to bathe in the springs of a lovely garden close by Aladdin's home. It was forbidden to look at the Princess as she passed by but Aladdin was filled with a desire to see her face. One day he hid behind the gate and caught a glimpse of her as she passed by.

The Princess was so beautiful that Aladdin fell in love with her there and then. He had to win her heart!

"The Princess would never marry you!" laughed his mother. "She will want to marry a rich Prince." But Aladdin begged her to visit the palace and ask the Sultan's permission.

"You can give him our jewels as a gift," he added.

When the Sultan saw the jewels his eyes lit up.

"Any man who owns such riches as these must be deserving of my daughter's hand," he said. But his chief minister, the Grand Vizier, was most displeased for he wanted the Princess to marry his own son.

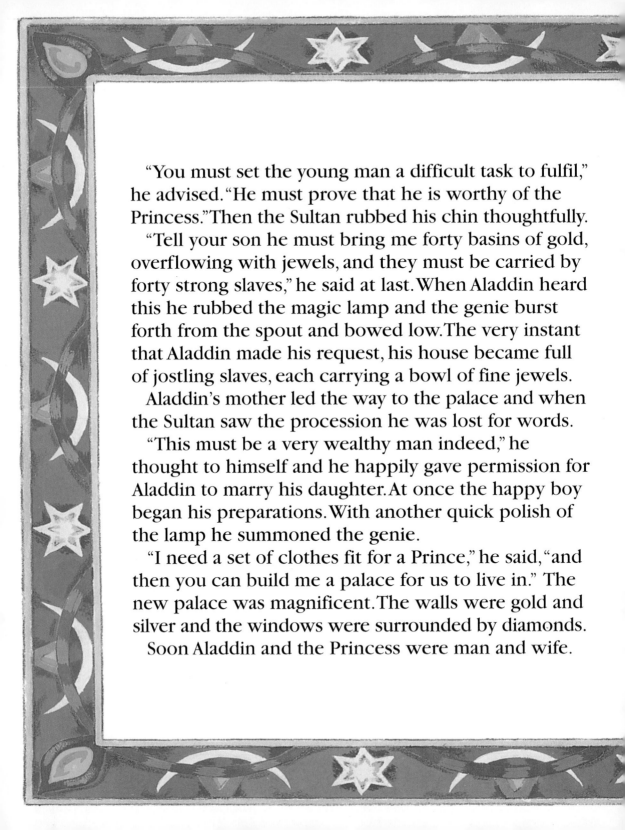

"You must set the young man a difficult task to fulfil," he advised. "He must prove that he is worthy of the Princess." Then the Sultan rubbed his chin thoughtfully.

"Tell your son he must bring me forty basins of gold, overflowing with jewels, and they must be carried by forty strong slaves," he said at last. When Aladdin heard this he rubbed the magic lamp and the genie burst forth from the spout and bowed low. The very instant that Aladdin made his request, his house became full of jostling slaves, each carrying a bowl of fine jewels.

Aladdin's mother led the way to the palace and when the Sultan saw the procession he was lost for words.

"This must be a very wealthy man indeed," he thought to himself and he happily gave permission for Aladdin to marry his daughter. At once the happy boy began his preparations. With another quick polish of the lamp he summoned the genie.

"I need a set of clothes fit for a Prince," he said, "and then you can build me a palace for us to live in." The new palace was magnificent. The walls were gold and silver and the windows were surrounded by diamonds.

Soon Aladdin and the Princess were man and wife.

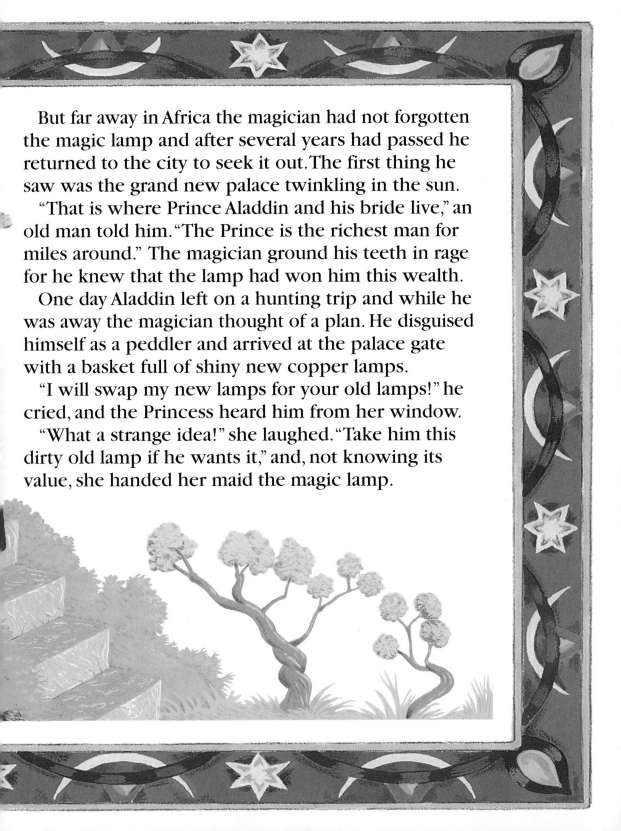

But far away in Africa the magician had not forgotten the magic lamp and after several years had passed he returned to the city to seek it out. The first thing he saw was the grand new palace twinkling in the sun.

"That is where Prince Aladdin and his bride live," an old man told him. "The Prince is the richest man for miles around." The magician ground his teeth in rage for he knew that the lamp had won him this wealth.

One day Aladdin left on a hunting trip and while he was away the magician thought of a plan. He disguised himself as a peddler and arrived at the palace gate with a basket full of shiny new copper lamps.

"I will swap my new lamps for your old lamps!" he cried, and the Princess heard him from her window.

"What a strange idea!" she laughed. "Take him this dirty old lamp if he wants it," and, not knowing its value, she handed her maid the magic lamp.

"Would you take this old lamp?" the maid asked the magician and the wicked man nearly shouted for joy. Quickly he grabbed the lamp and sped from the city. As night fell he rubbed the spout and roused the genie.

"Take the Princess and her palace back to Africa with me," he ordered, and in a flash it was done. The next day the Sultan was horrified to find that the palace and his beloved daughter had disappeared.

"Aladdin has tricked you!" cried the Grand Vizier. Then the enraged Sultan ordered that Aladdin be captured and put to death. When the townspeople heard the news they were angry and shouted out for Aladdin's release. The Sultan hesitated for the Prince was very popular. At last he decided to show mercy.

"I swear to you that I will find the Princess," the boy promised when he was found. "If I should fail then you can punish me however you like."

So Aladdin's life was spared and he left the city to seek his wife. But it was as if she had disappeared into thin air. No-one knew where she was and no-one could help him. Many days passed by and at last he threw himself on his knees and prayed. As he did so, he rubbed the magic ring he still wore on his finger. With a flash of light the genie appeared before him.

"Take me to the Princess," begged the delighted Aladdin and in a trice he found himself outside her window. Soon she was in his arms and telling him all that had happened. Then Aladdin understood. The Genie of the Lamp had a new master. Carefully he handed the Princess a small packet of powder.

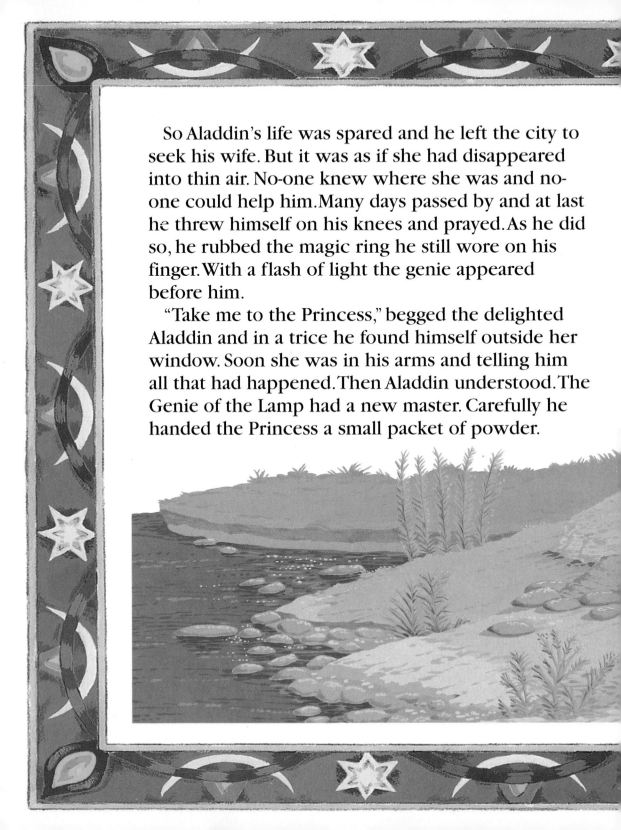

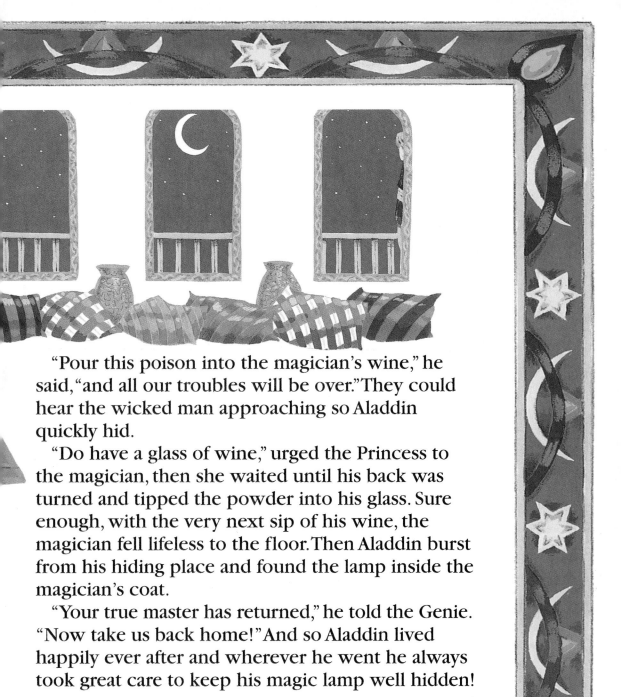

"Pour this poison into the magician's wine," he said, "and all our troubles will be over." They could hear the wicked man approaching so Aladdin quickly hid.

"Do have a glass of wine," urged the Princess to the magician, then she waited until his back was turned and tipped the powder into his glass. Sure enough, with the very next sip of his wine, the magician fell lifeless to the floor. Then Aladdin burst from his hiding place and found the lamp inside the magician's coat.

"Your true master has returned," he told the Genie. "Now take us back home!" And so Aladdin lived happily ever after and wherever he went he always took great care to keep his magic lamp well hidden!

Sinbad the Sailor

This is the story of Sinbad the Sailor and his many strange adventures across the far seas. His first voyage was on a merchant ship bound for the East Indies and one day it passed a peculiar little island. It was smooth and green and the Captain decided his sailors could go ashore and stretch their legs. But when the cook lit a fire the earth began to tremble beneath their feet and to their horror, the whole island rose up out of the water and everyone was thrown into the sea.

"It is a whale!" shouted the Captain. "Swim for the ship!" He quickly weighed anchor and set sail, but one sailor was left behind and that was Sinbad! He clung to a piece of driftwood and watched as the ship slowly disappeared from sight. Two days passed before the waves pushed him close to the shores of an island.

Soon he was lying upon dry land.

"I must find water and food," he gasped and set off into the forest that bordered the beach. He had not gone far when he found an extraordinary white dome lying upon the ground. What could it be?

Just then Sinbad heard the flapping of wings high above him and glancing up he saw the most enormous bird. It was a Roc and the strange dome must surely be the Roc's egg! Sure enough she landed close by and sat down upon her nest. Then Sinbad had an idea.

"If I tie myself to her foot I may be able to escape from this island," he thought and he quickly wrapped his turban around one huge claw. At daybreak the Roc stood up and with a mighty cry took off into the sky. She flew over sea, then over land and at last swooped down and came to rest in a deep valley. Sinbad hastily untied himself and looked around.

To his amazement he found the ground was covered with glittering diamonds. Just then Sinbad heard a hiss and spinning around he saw six large serpents slithering across the rocks towards him. He turned and ran and at last found a hiding place in a hole in the ground. There he hid all that day and all through the night and at last the serpents gave up and crawled away.

Suddenly a a huge lump of meat fell on the ground in front of him. Then another, and another. With a loud flapping of wings a great eagle landed on one large piece of meat and took off into the air again. Sinbad remembered a story he had heard about the men who lived in these parts. They had devised a special way of gathering diamonds. They threw meat down into the valley and the jewels would stick to the soft flesh. Then the eagles would grab the meat and fly with it to their nests. There the hunters picked the diamonds from the meat and so both eagles and men were happy! Quickly Sinbad tied himself to a piece of meat. This could be his way out of the valley! Sure enough, an eagle took the meat and flew off to his nest. What a shock the hunter got to see a man landing there!

From the mountain top Sinbad found his way to the coast and set sail once again but this time his ship was blown off course by a violent wind. They came close to an island and saw to their horror that the sea was full of strange monkey-like creatures swimming towards them. Soon they were crawling on the decks and swarming up the rigging.

The Ape Men took over the ship and forced Sinbad
and his shipmates to jump overboard and swim for
land. They set off to explore the island and soon found
a deserted palace. In the courtyard was a huge mound
of what looked suspiciously like human bones but the
men were so tired that they decided to rest there for
the night. Suddenly a loud roar filled the air and in
through the gate strode the most horrible one-eyed
ogre. The sailors sat rooted to the spot.

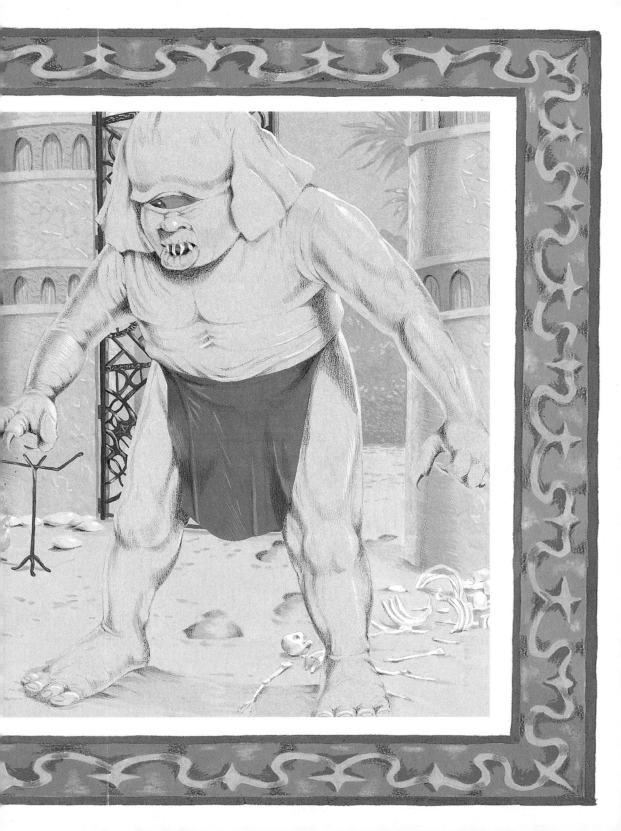

The beast plucked up one sailor and while the others watched in horror, roasted him on a spit and with much smacking of lips, ate him! Then the ogre fell asleep and his huge body blocked the gateway.

"We must try and kill him," whispered Sinbad. "If we take the red hot spits from the fire and push them in his eye he will surely die." So they crept up on the giant as he lay on his back and thrust the iron poles into his eye. The giant howled with pain and the sailors quickly made their escape. But the ogre was not dead and he chased them through the jungle and down to the beach. The terrified men leapt into the sea and swam for their lives while the ogre threw huge boulders after them. Many perished but lucky Sinbad survived with two other sailors.

At last the waves threw them upon another island and there another danger awaited them. A giant green lizard crept from the bushes and before they knew what was upon them, had gobbled down Sinbad's companions. Clever Sinbad lit a circle of fire around a tall tree then climbed into its branches. That night he was safe from the fearsome beast.

The next morning he saw a ship sail close by and, jumping from the tree he ran into the sea, shouting at the top of his voice. To his great relief, the Captain heard him and had soon pulled him on board.

After this Sinbad spent some time at home but after many months had passed he set sail once again. This time the ship ran out of food and the hungry sailors landed upon an unknown shore and set off in search of something to eat. To their delight they found a baby Roc hatching from its huge shell.

"Do not touch it!" cried Sinbad. "The mother Roc is a huge bird and will surely kill you," but the sailors paid him no heed and soon the infant Roc was roasting over a fire. Then the sky above them went dark and looking up, the sailors were horrified to see both mother and father Roc returning to their egg.

"To the ship! To the ship!" they cried as they ran pell mell down the beach. Soon the ship was fleeing the island, but the Rocs were in full pursuit. They bore huge rocks which they dropped upon the hapless sailors and soon the sea was full of drowning men. Good fortune was smiling again on Sinbad, for he was the only survivor.

At last the sea cast him upon an island and Sinbad set off to explore inland. He had not gone far when he came upon an old man sitting beside a brook.

"Please carry me across to the fruit trees on the other side," asked the old man pitifully. Sinbad gladly obliged but was shocked to find that the old man wrapped his legs around Sinbad's neck so strongly that he nearly passed out and at last fell down upon the ground. Then the old man gave him a mighty kick in the ribs and forced him up and onwards. All that day the old man ate fruit after fruit and at night he slept with his legs still locked tightly around Sinbad's head.

So it went on, day after day, and at last Sinbad thought of a plan. He squeezed a good amount of grape juice into an empty gourd and left it in the sun. After a while the juice turned into wine and Sinbad offered it to the old man.

"This is good," said the old man, swallowing it eagerly, and soon the gourd was empty. But the old man was drunk and danced so happily upon Sinbad's shoulders that he soon fell off! So at last Sinbad was free. Once again he hailed a passing ship and scrambled aboard.

After a time the ship landed at an island well
known for its wonderful coconuts.

"This is how you gather them," a rich merchant
told Sinbad. "Just copy me." Then he began throwing
stones at the monkeys who clustered around the nuts
at the top of the palm trees. The angry monkeys
grabbed the nearest missiles to hand and soon
coconuts were raining down upon the ground!

Sinbad traded his coconuts for spices and silks on
his voyage around the islands but his next journey
was to end once again in calamity. His ship was
caught in a strong current which dragged it upon
sharp rocks and the sailors were cast screaming
overboard.

Sinbad found himself the sole survivor upon that
rocky coast but there seemed to be no escape.

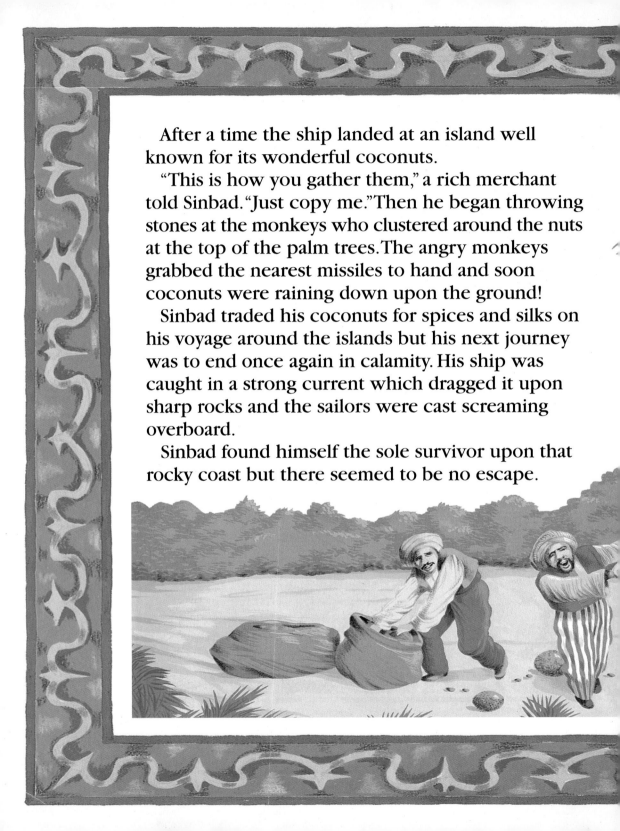

At last he found a small channel cut through the sheer rock face where the sea had forced a passage inland. He made himself a raft and, lashing himself to the timbers, set sail under the mountain. The current carried him through the dark for many hours but at last he emerged into bright sunshine and was found by a group of natives. They led him before their King and soon Sinbad was recounting his many exciting voyages to far off lands. The King was fascinated.

"Please return to your Sultan with gifts from the island of Serendib," he said, "but be sure to return soon for I would dearly love to hear more of your adventures."

So Sinbad arrived home with many costly presents which the Sultan was well pleased to receive.

"Now you must visit the King again," the Sultan told Sinbad. "We must repay his generosity with gifts of our own." So it was that Sinbad returned to the island of Serendib and was treated like a royal visitor.

At last he made his final farewells and set sail for home. He was getting old and wished to spend the rest of his days in the safe harbour of his house, surrounded by loving family and friends. The voyages of Sinbad the Sailor were over!

OTHER TITLES IN THIS SERIES INCLUDE:

AESOP'S FABLES
⚬
GRIMM'S FAIRYTALES
⚬
HANS ANDERSEN'S FAIRYTALES
⚬
JUST-SO STORIES
⚬
NURSERY TALES
⚬
TALES OF BRER RABBIT
⚬
WIND IN THE WILLOWS